# OFFICIAL STICKER BOOK

## By Courtney Carbone

Designed by Stephanie Sumulong

Random House  New York

TM & © 2019 Nintendo. All rights reserved. Published in the United States by Random House Children's Books, a division of Penguin Random House LLC, 1745 Broadway, New York, NY 10019, and in Canada by Penguin Random House Canada Limited, Toronto. Random House and the colophon are registered trademarks of Penguin Random House LLC.

rhcbooks.com

ISBN 978-1-5247-7262-8

MANUFACTURED IN CHINA

10 9 8 7 6 5 4

# Welcome to Animal Crossing

Animal Crossing is an exciting world where you get to create your own town. Build a home, make friends, collect items, and have fun!

How many words can you make out of

# NEW LEAF?

See pages 63–64 for all answers.

# CONGRATULATIONS!

The town's citizens have declared you the new mayor! Are you up for the challenge?
To get started, write your name on the sign.
Then name your new town!

Your Name

Town Name

**TIP:**
Can't think of anything? Try adding your name or a favorite thing to one of the words or suffixes below.

-wood   Land   Forest
City   Hollow   Township
Village   Borough
Nook   Rock   Point
Landing   Town
-topia   -ville   Park

# TOWN FLAG

You'll need a flag to hang in the center of town to inspire your fellow citizens.

**Design your town flag!**

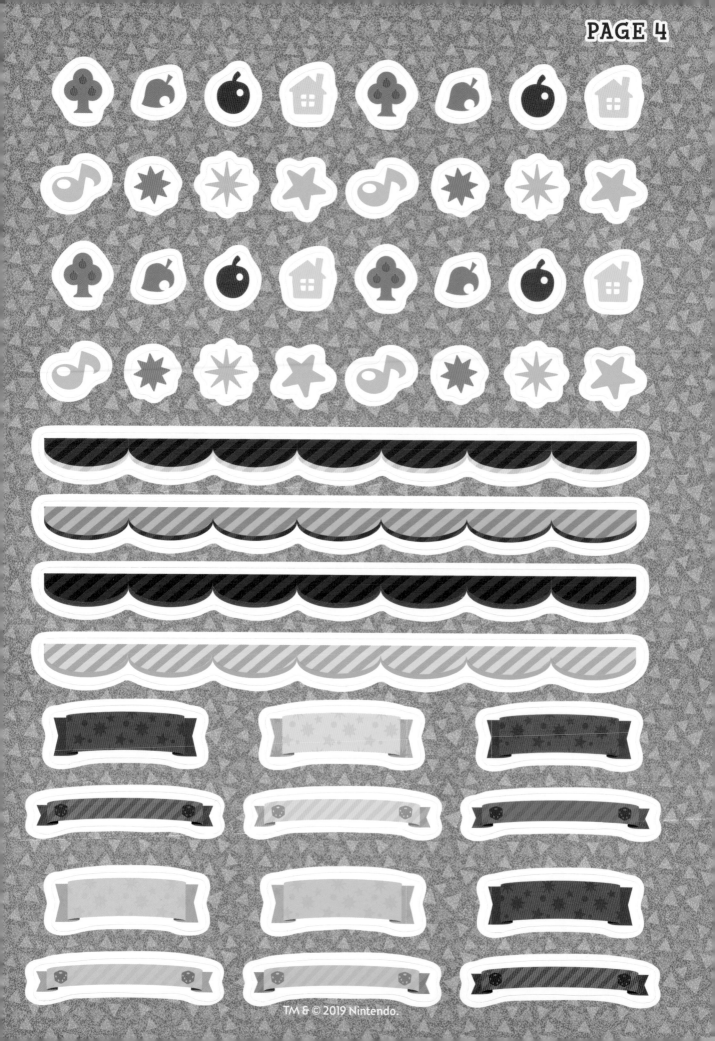

As mayor, you'll need to pay close attention to details.

**Practice your skills by identifying ten differences between these two pictures.**

5

# MEET ISABELLE!

Isabelle the dog keeps things running smoothly at Town Hall.
She assists the town mayor.
She is very helpful and friendly.

# PICTURE-PERFECT!

Everyone needs a Town Pass card for identification and travel purposes.
Fill out your card. Make sure to add a picture of yourself!
Then create a few cards for your friends.

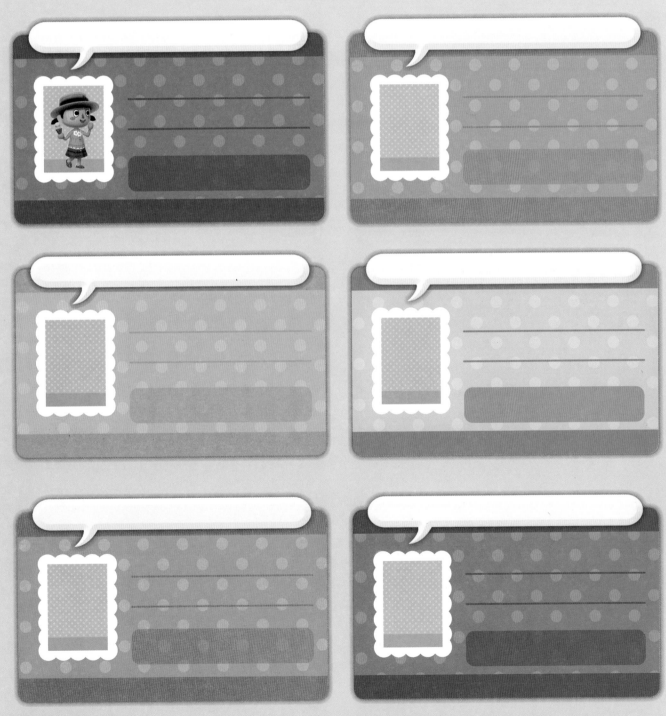

# HOME, SWEET HOME!

Before you can start your life in town, you will need a place to live.
Draw your new house. Then use your stickers to add characters and furniture to your new home.

**Did you Know?**
You can live in a tent on your property until your house is finished!

# MAP TIME!

Create a map of your town so visitors can find their way around.
Use your stickers to add buildings, bridges, trees, and bodies of water.

# WELCOME!

There are lots of ways to make
your home more comfortable.

**Add furniture and decorations to create a special place you can call home.**

# DESIGN TIME!

Now that your home is all set up, it's time to show your unique style!
Create your own wallpaper patterns and floor designs.

# BREAKING GROUND

The citizens of your town want to celebrate your
new leadership by planting a tree in your honor.
Over time, the tree will grow big and strong, just like your town!

**Add leaf stickers to help your tree grow.
Then decorate the scene with lots of character stickers.**

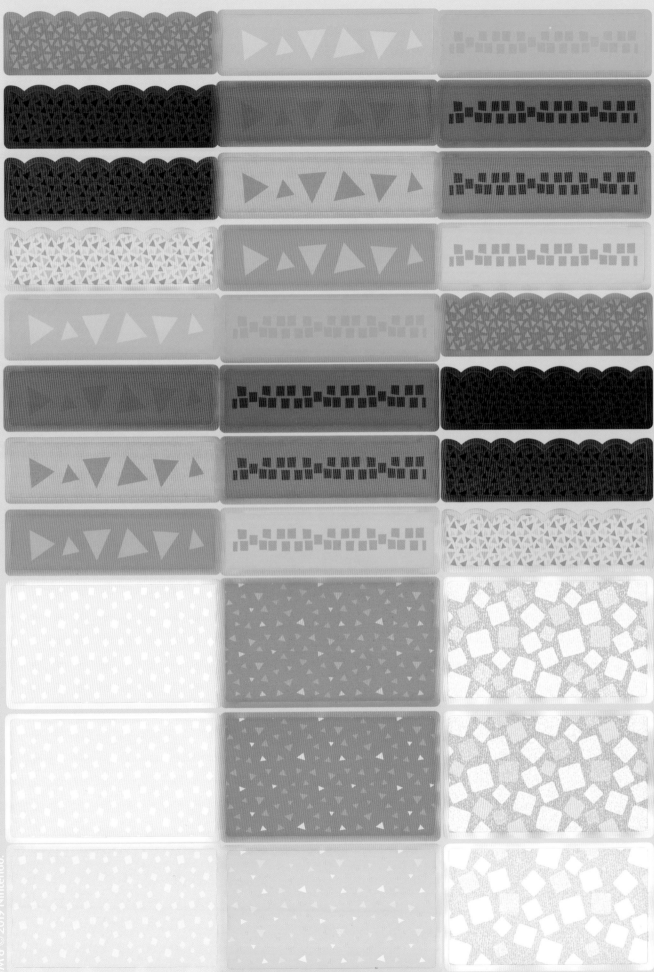

# SPECIAL ANNOUNCEMENT!

The citizens of your town post messages on the bulletin board near the train station.

**What message would you like to share with the town? Write it below.**

# HAPPY HOMES

Digby the dog runs the Happy Home Showcase.
Use the key to color Digby.

**Did you Know?**
Digby and Isabelle are twins!

**KEY**
1 = brown
2 = gray
3 = white
4 = red
5 = blue
6 = black
7 = yellow

# FUN WITH FRUIT!

There are lots of trees all over your town, including fruit trees. Look at the patterns below. Figure out what the next two fruits in each row should be, and use your stickers to fill them in.

# BEE CAREFUL!

You can shake trees to see if something useful is hiding in the branches.
But be careful—some trees are home to nests full of bumblebees!
Escape the angry swarm by finding a path that leads you safely home.

A  B  C  D  E

# SEASHELL SEARCH!

It's a lovely day to collect seashells.
Use your stickers to finish the puzzle.
Fill in the grid so the seashell, conch,
sand dollar, and coral pictures appear
only once in each row, column,
and box of four squares.

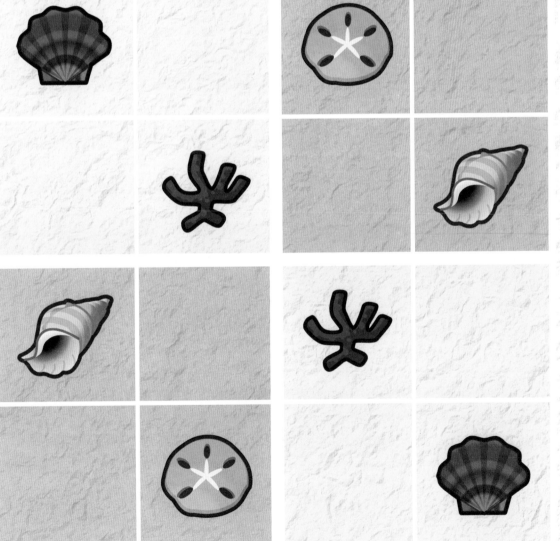

# GARDEN PARTY!

Flowers are sprouting up all over town!
Match your stickers with their shapes
to learn the names of all the flowers.

carnation

cosmo

dandelion

Jacob's ladder

lily

pansy

rose

tulip

violet

18

# FOSSIL FIND!

There are many prehistoric fossils waiting to be discovered in your town.
Find these fossilized creatures in the puzzle.

APATOSAURUS    ARCHELON    DIMETRODON
IGUANODON    MAMMOTH    PARASAUR
STEGOSAUR    TRICERATOPS    VELOCIRAPTOR

| P | D | C | A | R | A | E | T | O | C | H | N | M | E | V |
|---|---|---|---|---|---|---|---|---|---|---|---|---|---|---|
| L | E | F | H | Y | E | C | V | B | Y | E | W | Q | X | S |
| D | A | P | A | T | O | S | A | U | R | U | S | R | W | P |
| V | R | Y | N | E | B | C | D | T | Y | O | P | E | C | O |
| I | C | D | I | M | E | T | R | O | D | O | N | Y | V | T |
| N | H | L | G | A | U | I | P | O | L | R | E | U | D | A |
| G | E | Z | U | M | Y | P | O | E | T | U | F | J | S | R |
| H | L | K | A | M | R | A | C | D | F | R | C | M | O | E |
| W | O | J | N | O | F | R | L | W | R | G | Y | K | P | C |
| A | N | E | O | T | V | A | L | P | E | Y | H | I | E | I |
| Q | H | D | D | H | E | S | T | E | G | O | S | A | U | R |
| X | F | C | O | H | L | A | I | Q | S | E | R | E | M | T |
| S | M | B | N | U | I | U | Z | W | D | J | I | D | X | R |
| V | E | L | O | C | I | R | A | P | T | O | R | C | W | S |
| R | K | P | W | L | A | K | C | E | S | D | C | E | D | K |

# THE GOOD LIFE

You will need special currency to buy things around town. To find out what the townsfolk use to buy and sell items, connect the dots in the picture and identify the shape.

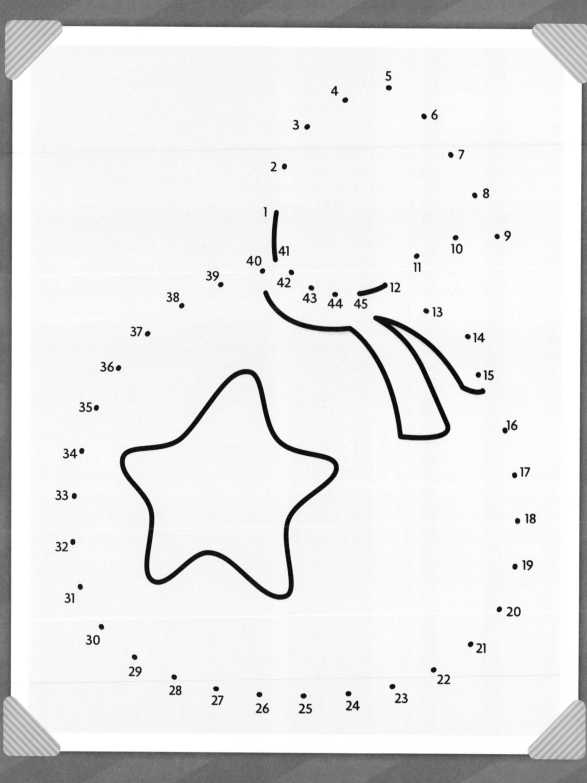

PAGE 17

PAGE 18

PAGE 25

TM & © 2019 Nintendo.

# NOOK'S HOMES

Can you find the shortest way to Nook's Homes?

# TWO OF A KIND

Timmy and Tommy are raccoon twins who run Tom Nook's general store.
They look and dress alike, so it's hard to tell them apart!

**Look closely at the raccoon pairs.
Find the pair that perfectly matches the picture at the top.**

# WALK THIS WAY

Use your stickers to complete the puzzle of Kicks in front of his shoe store.
Then unscramble the letters below and write the name on the store.

KKCSI

# SEEING DOUBLE

Kicks the skunk sells shoes at Kicks.
Draw his other half so he can get back to work.
Use the picture at the top for help.

# FLOWER POWER!

In the town gardening center, you can buy flowers, trees, and planting supplies.
Which of your favorite flowers would you buy from the store?

# GREEN THUMB

Leif is a sloth who runs the town gardening center.
Use the grid to help you draw him. Then color your picture to match the original.

# SHOP TILL YOU DROP!

Re-Tail is a recycling center where you can buy and sell goods.
Use your stickers to show what else you can find in the recycling center.

# A PERFECT PAIR

Cyrus and Reese are the husband-and-wife team who run Re-Tail.
To find out what kind of animal they are, replace each letter below with the
one that comes before it in the alphabet and write them on the blanks.

# B M Q B D B

......... ......... ......... ......... ......... .........

# FASHION FUN

Able Sisters is a store where you can buy clothing and accessories. Use your clothing stickers to show what you would buy at the store.

# SEWING SISTERS

Sable and Mabel are the sisters who work at the Able Sisters shop.
Help them with their tailoring by connecting the dots to complete the clothing patterns.

# STYLE ICON

A very fashionable hedgehog sells accessories in the Able Sisters shop.
To find out her name, use the key.

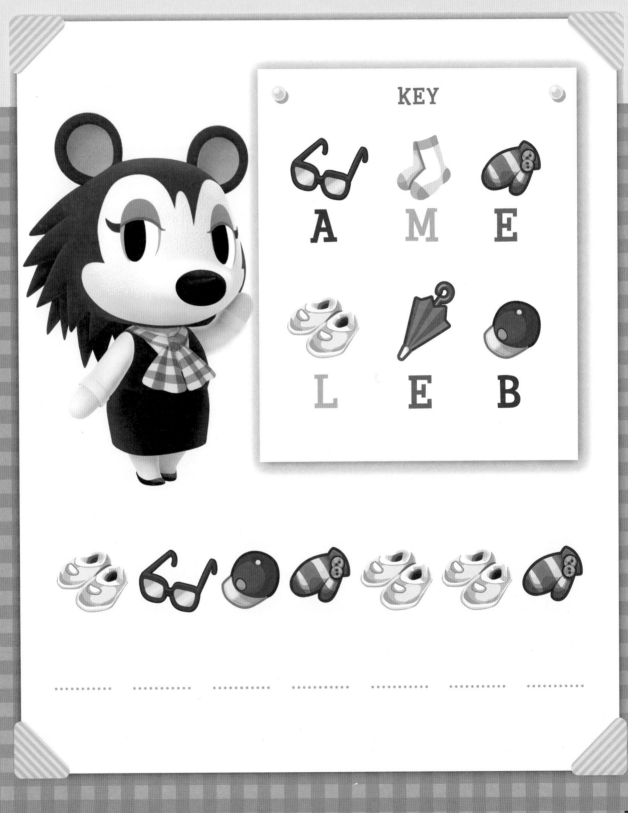

KEY

A    M    E

L    E    B

.......... .......... .......... .......... .......... .......... ..........

# DRESS TO IMPRESS

Get yourself some custom clothing!
Match the shadows of the shirt, dress, shoes, socks, hat, and
accessories with your stickers to show off your fashion sense.

# ALL MIXED UP!

Harriet the pink poodle is the town hairstylist.
To find out the name of her salon, cross out each letter of the alphabet that appears in order.
Write the remaining letters on the blanks.

A S B H C D
A E F G M H I
J K L P M N
O P O Q R S
O T U V D W
L X E Y Z

# NEW LEAF, NEW LOOK!

It's time for your hair appointment!
Draw yourself with a new hairstyle.

# COFFEE BREAK

The town café is the perfect place to drink coffee, meet friends, or even get a part-time job!
To find out what the café is called, start at the arrow and, going clockwise
around the circle, write every third letter in order on the blanks.

# ALL OVER TOWN

Your town could benefit from some new items!

Use your stickers to add trees, flowers, a bench, a fountain, and more to the scene!

# MUSEUM MYSTERY

Blathers the owl is director of the town museum.
Unscramble the words to find out what visitors can see in his museum.

1. SHFI

2. ICSNSTE

3. LSOSFSI

4. RAKWRTO

1. ........ ........ ........ ........

2. ........ ........ ........ ........ ........

3. ........ ........ ........ ........ ........

4. ........ ........ ........ ........ ........

# PLAYTIME!

With a friend, take turns connecting two dots with a straight line. If the line you draw completes a box, write your initials in it and take another turn. Count one point for squares containing your initials. Count three points for every box that contains a Play Coin. When all the dots have been connected, count how many points each player has.

## Whoever has more points wins!

# GOOD FORTUNE

You can use your Play Coins to buy fortune cookies in town,
which may contain tickets you can exchange for special items.

**Write your own fortunes!**

# NEED A HAND?

There are lots of useful tools to help you around town.
Use the clues to learn about some of them.

1. ........ ........ ........ ........ ........ ........ ........ ........   ........ ........ ........

Clue: It is essential for catching fish.

2. ........ ........ ........ ........ ........ ........ ........ ........

Clue: It allows you to dig for fossils.

3. ........ ........ ........

Clue: It helps you cut wood.

4. ........ ........ ........ ........ ........ ........ ........ ........ ........ ........

Clue: It's used to shoot stones far distances.

5. ........ ........ ........

Clue: It allows you to catch insects.

6. ........ ........ ........ ........ ........ ........ ........   ........ ........ ........

Clue: It helps you tend your garden.

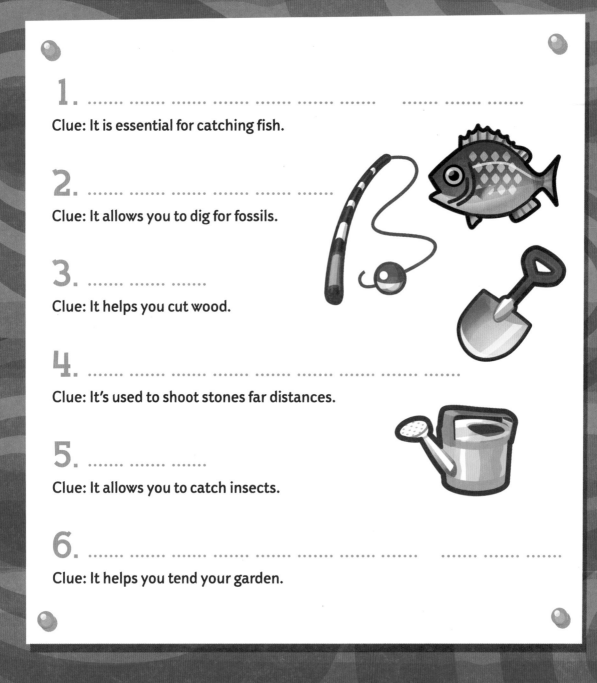

# LOST AND FOUND

Can you help the citizens of your town find the items they're missing?
You'll know what to look for by reading the backward words below.

1. Y R E N O I T A T S
   ........................

2. A L L E R B M U
   ........................

3. E V I H E E B
   ........................

4. T R I H S
   ........................

5. L E V O H S
   ........................

# CREATIVE CANVAS

Crazy Redd sells works of art from a tent in the middle of town.
Create your own masterpiece!

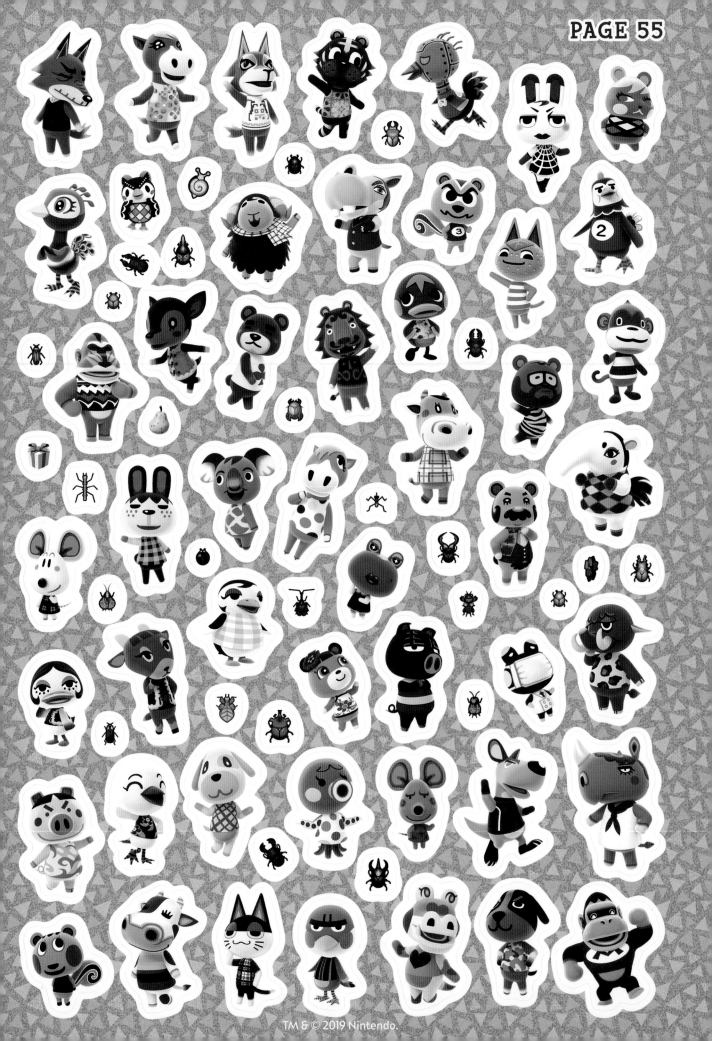

# GAME TIME!

The animals in your town love to play hide-and-seek.
See if you can find them!

# GONE FISHING!

There are lots of different kinds of fish in the rivers, lakes, and ponds in your town. Find the path of fish that goes all the way from START to FINISH. Go back if frogs, turtles, lobsters, or any other kinds of sea creatures are blocking your path!

START

FINISH

# FUN IN THE SUN!

Looking to get out of town?
Use the code to discover the home of the former mayor!

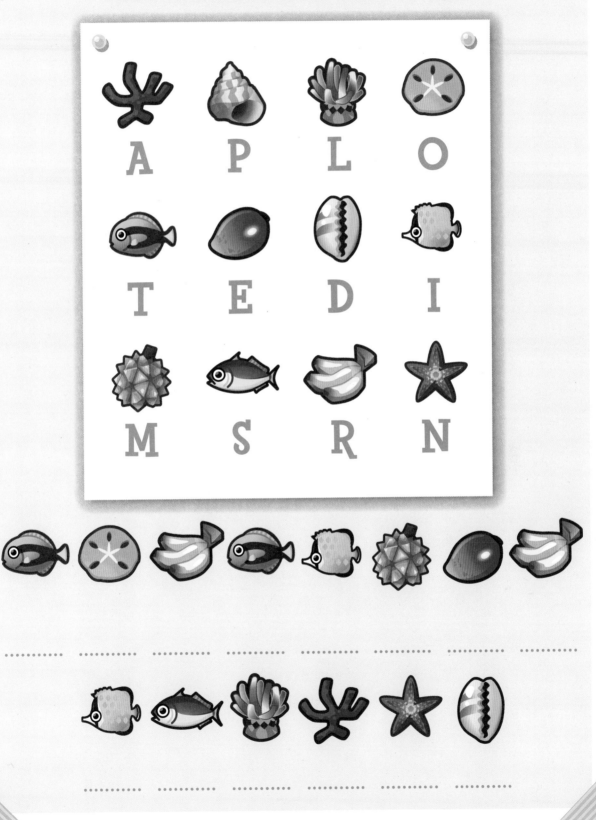

# BUG COLLECTOR

Nets are helpful for catching the many different types of bugs on Tortimer Island.
Use your stickers to match the pattern in the first box.

48

# STRIKE A POSE!

One way to capture your memories with friends around town is by taking pictures.
Use the character stickers of your favorite friends.

# SOMETHING SPECIAL

One of your responsibilities as mayor is to commission
public-works projects to improve and expand the town,
such as a new office building, a park, or a science museum.
What new building or facility would you like to add to your town? Draw it!

# LAWS OF THE LAND

As mayor, you have the power to pass town
ordinances—the laws that all citizens must follow.
Here are four examples of ordinances. Match each one with its description.

1. Keep Your Town Beautiful

2. Early Bird

3. Night Owl

4. Bell Boom

A. Creates more wealth to go around town.

B. Allows shops to open early in the morning.

C. Protects nature and keeps garbage
off the streets.

D. Requires shops to stay open late at night.

## What other ordinances will you create for your town?

........................................................................................

........................................................................................

........................................................................................

........................................................................................

**TIP:**
Remember, the sky's
the limit! (Unless you
create an ordinance
that says it is not!)

# SEASON'S GREETINGS!

Your town is a wonderful place to live all year round.

## Use your stickers to create a fun scene for each of the seasons!

Which season is your favorite?

# CELEBRATE!

Balloons can often be found during special celebrations.
How many balloons can you count below?

**HINT:**
Write a number on
each balloon so you
don't lose count.

# AFTER DARK

Looking for a night out? Check out Club LOL, the town nightclub.
Use your stickers to add friends to the scene.

KK

**TIP:** Be careful not to make the club too crowded!

# SMOOTH SOUNDS

K.K. Slider is the musical entertainment for Club LOL.
Help him entertain his guests by creating your own song!
Use your stickers to add musical notes, and write your own lyrics.

**TIP:**
Tip: Need help coming up with a song? Try writing about the time of year, fun activities with your friends, or something special about your town!

# LOOKING FOR A LAUGH

Dr. Shrunk is Club LOL's owner—and a retired stand-up comedian!
He writes lots of jokes. Can you guess the answers to his riddles?

**Q.** What song should they play at Kicks shoe store?

1. .............................................................................................

**Q.** Why is the town currency called Bells?

2. .............................................................................................

**Q.** Why did Leif the sloth close the gardening center early?

3. .............................................................................................

**Q.** Why didn't Blathers want more insects for his museum?

4. .............................................................................................

# WHAT'S UP?

Everyone likes to hear what's going on in town.
Write in the bubbles to create your own comic strip!

# WELCOME, EVERYONE!

As mayor, you can invite friends from other towns to visit you.

**Who would you like to invite to your town?**

...................................................................

...................................................................

...................................................................

...................................................................

...................................................................

...................................................................

**What would you like to do with your friends while they are visiting?**

...................................................................

...................................................................

...................................................................

...................................................................

...................................................................

...................................................................

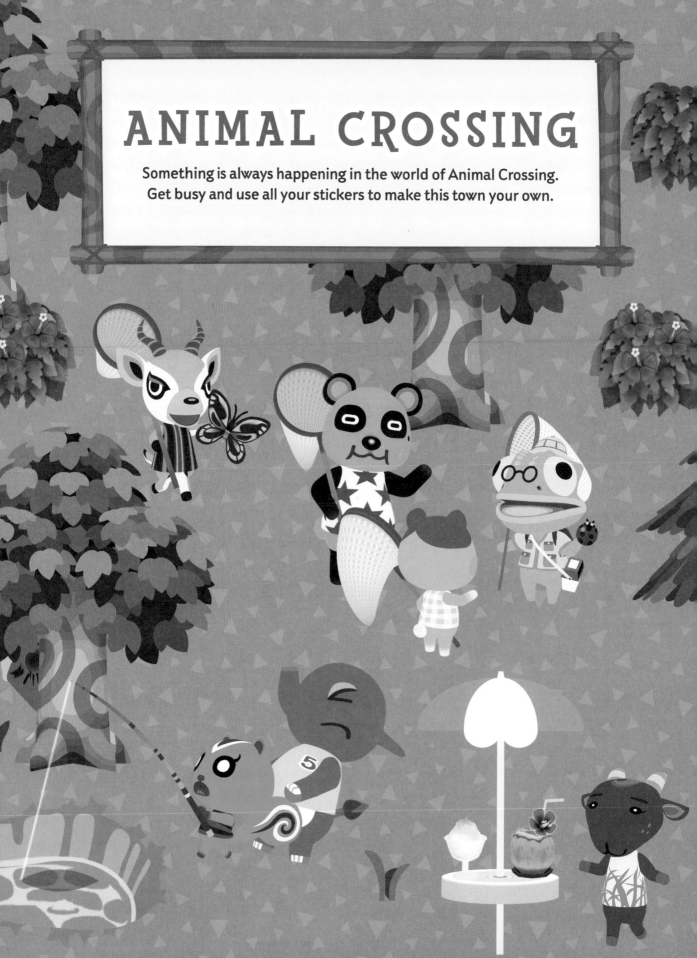

# ANIMAL CROSSING

Something is always happening in the world of Animal Crossing.
Get busy and use all your stickers to make this town your own.

# ANSWERS

**PAGE 2:** An, eel, ewe, feel, few, flea, flew, lawn, leaf, lean, new, wane, we, and wean.

**PAGE 5**

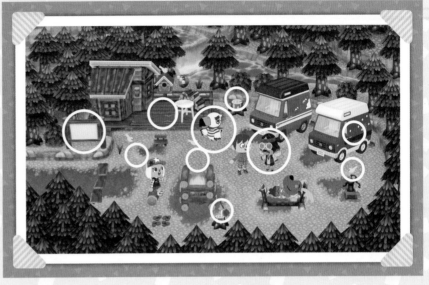

**PAGE 15**

**PAGE 16: C.**

**PAGE 17**

**PAGE 19**

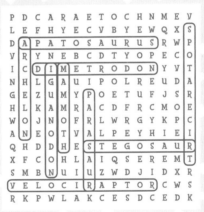

**PAGE 21**

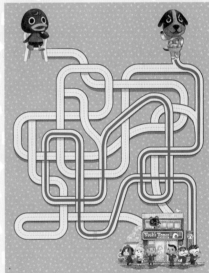

**PAGE 22: C.**

**PAGE 23: KICKS.**

**PAGE 28: Alpaca.**

**PAGE 31: Labelle.**

**PAGE 33: Shampoodle.**

**PAGE 35: The Roost.**

**PAGE 37:** 1. fish, 2. insects, 3. fossils, and 4. artwork.

**PAGE 40: Pelly, Phyllis, and Pete.**

**PAGE 42:** 1. fishing rod, 2. shovel, 3. axe, 4. slingshot, 5. net, and 6. watering can.

**PAGE 43:** 1. stationery, 2. umbrella, 3. beehive, 4. shirt, and 5. shovel.

# ANSWERS

**PAGE 45**

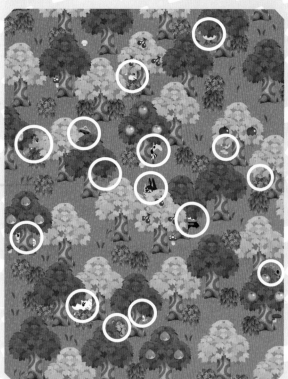

**PAGE 46**

**PAGE 47:** Tortimer Island.

**PAGE 48**

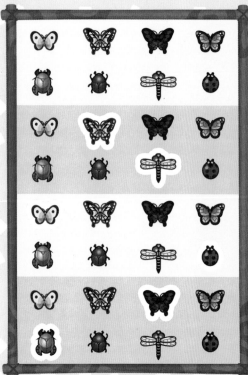

**PAGE 51:** 1-C, 2-B, 3-D, and 4-A.

**PAGE 54:** 35.

**PAGE 57:**
1. Heart and *Sole*.
2. The word has a nice *ring* to it.
3. Business had been *slow* all day.
4. They were starting to *bug* him!